P9-DIG-105

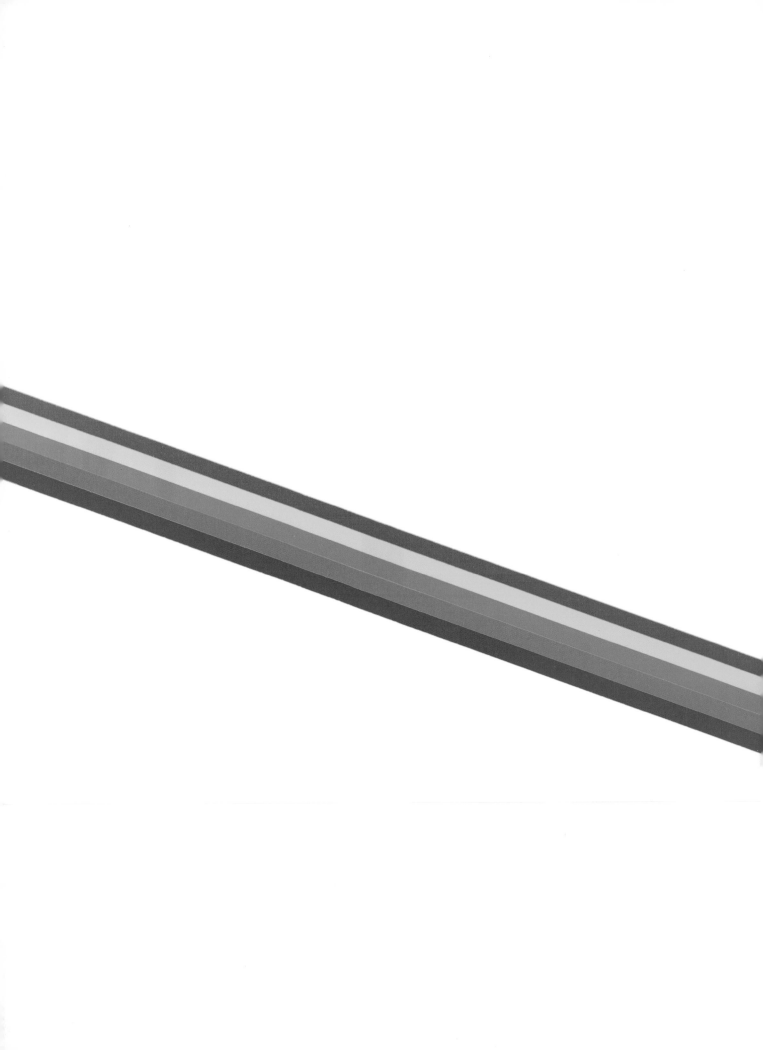

ABRAMS BOOKS FOR YOUNG READERS presents...

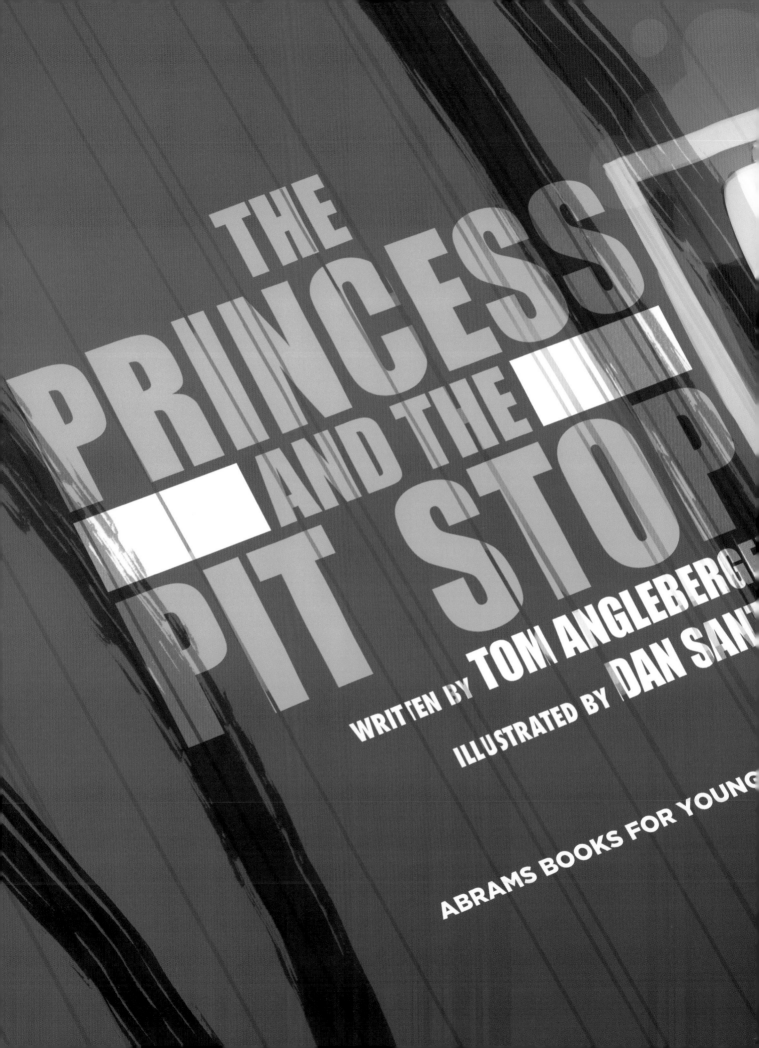

THE PRINCESS AND THE PIT STOP

WRITTEN BY **TOM ANGLEBERGER**

ILLUSTRATED BY **DAN SANTAT**

ABRAMS BOOKS FOR YOUNG

Once upon a time, there was a Princess who made a pit stop. While the Birds and Beasts changed her tires, her Fairy Godmother told her she was in last place!

With just one lap left!

499/500

SHE MIGHT AS WELL GIVE UP!

Instead, the Princess hit the gas!

She roared down the straightaway, running the Three Bears off the road!

She drove right over Tom Thumb and right under the Giant.

She beat
Jack and Jill
down the Hill . . .

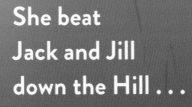

and passed Little Jack Horner in the Corner.

She blew the doors off the Big Bad Wolf and smoked the Three Little Pigs.

She charged past the Knight . . .

She outraced the Tortoise . . . AND the Hare.

and cut off the Dragon.

She honked at the Golden Goose,

blew a kiss to the Ugly Duckling,

then screeched past Four and Twenty Blackbirds.

She made the Seven Dwarfs grumpy
and left Snow White in a cloud of dust.

They all tried to beat her!
But the Cobbler got clobbered,

and Little Boy
Blue blew it.

And the Gingerbread Man admitted,

SHE **CAN** CATCH ME!

Little Bo Peep and her Sheep tried to stay with her, but the Princess lost 'em!

BO PEEP

when they got scared and hit the brakes . . .

THE PRINCESS JUST STEPPED ON THE GAS!

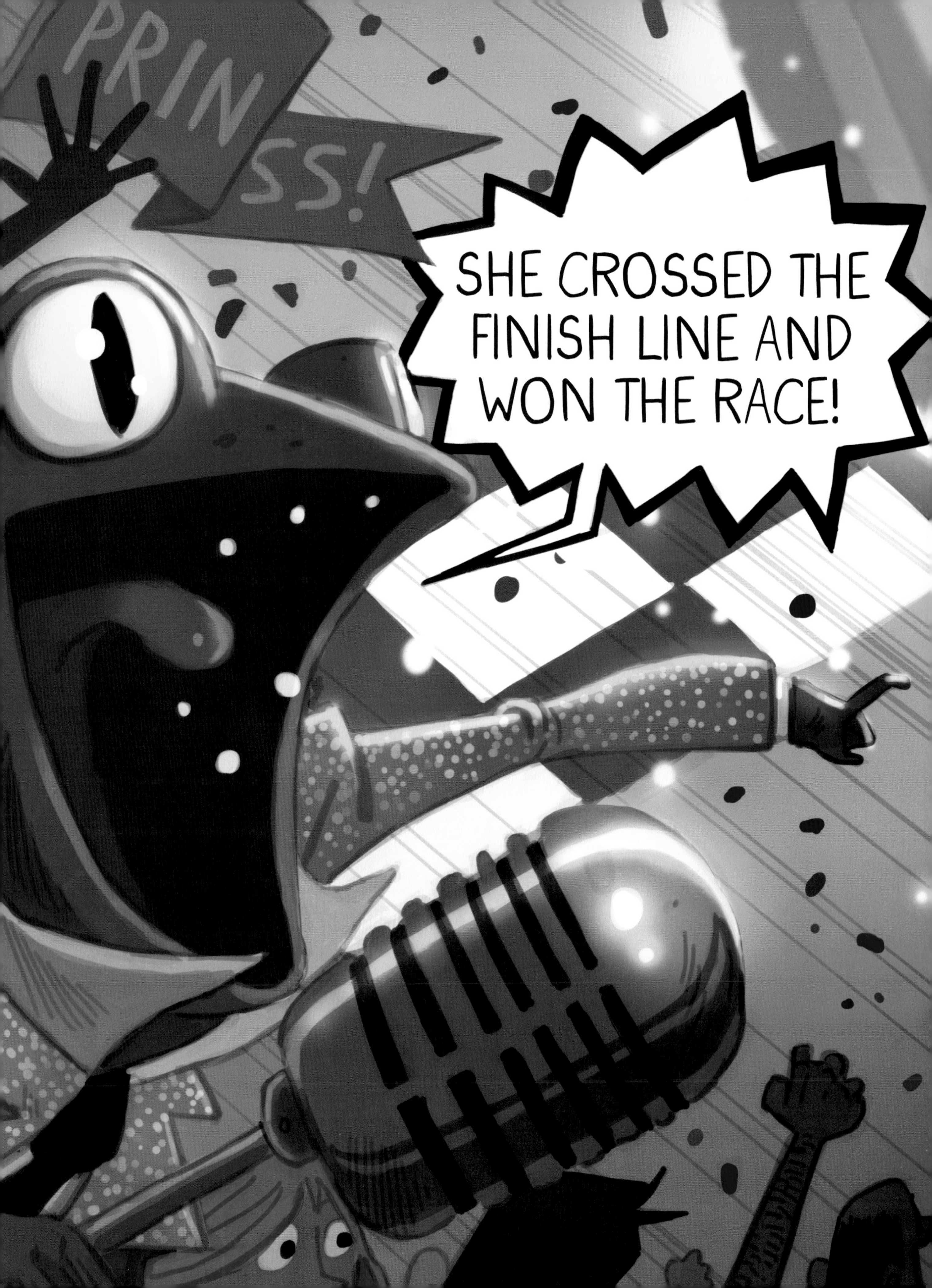
PRIN
SS!
SHE CROSSED THE FINISH LINE AND WON THE RACE!

She spun donuts on the track,

grabbed her trophy,

posed for pictures,

made a commercial,

and invited everybody to a big ball at the castle later.

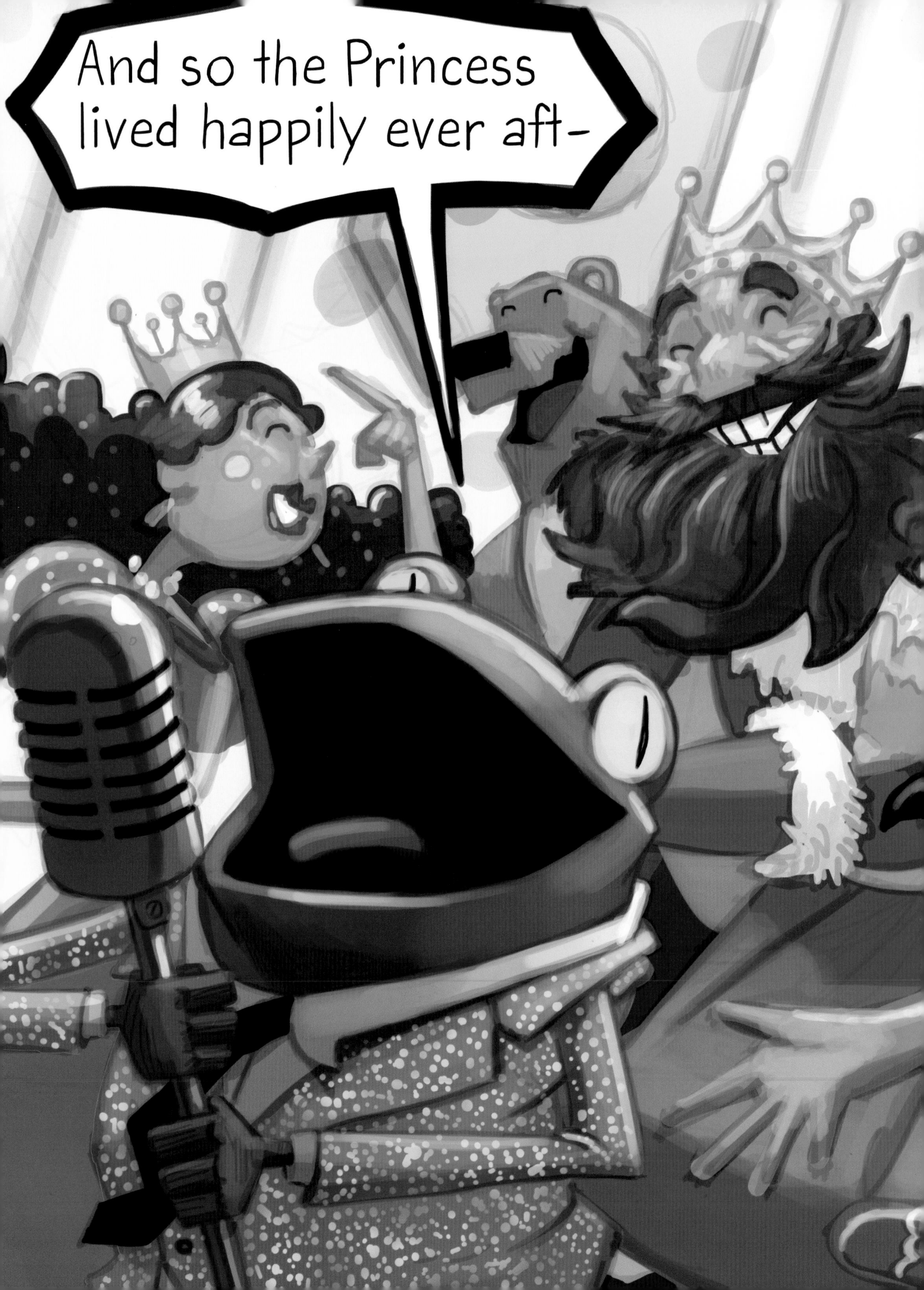
And so the Princess lived happily ever aft-

The End

Cataloging-in-Publication Data has been applied for and may
be obtained from the Library of Congress.

ISBN 978-1-4197-2848-8

Text copyright © 2018 Tom Angleberger

Illustrations copyright © 2018 Dan Santat

Book design by Chad W. Beckerman

Printed and bound in U.S.A.

10 9 8 7 6 5 4 3 2

Abrams Books for Young Readers are available at special discounts when purchased
in quantity for premiums and promotions as well as fundraising or educational
use. Special editions can also be created to specification. For details, contact
specialsales@abramsbooks.com or the address below.

ABRAMS The Art of Books
195 Broadway, New York, NY 10007
abramsbooks.com